Published by Caroline House
Boyds Mills Press, Inc.
A Highlights Company
815 Church Street
Honesdale, Pennsylvania 18431
Printed in China

Publisher Cataloging-in-Publication Data
Wahl, Jan
Cabbage moon / by Jan Wahl ; illustrated by Arden
Johnson-Petrov.—1st.ed.
[32] p. : col. ill.: cm.
Summary: When the unscrupulous Mr. Squink steals the moon
from the sky, Jennie the dog comes running to the rescue.
ISBN 1-56397-584-X
1. Moon—Fiction—Juvenile literature. 2. Sky—Fiction—Juvenile
literature. [1. Moon—Fiction. 2. Sky—Fiction.] I. Johnson-
Petrov, Arden, ill. II. Title.
[E]—dc21   1998   AC   CIP
Library of Congress Catalog Card Number 97-77734

First edition, 1998
Book designed by Tim Gillner and Arden Johnson-Petrov
The text of this book is set in 22-point New Baskerville.
The illustrations are done in pastels.

10 9 8 7 6 5 4 3 2 1

To Silky Sullivan,
who knows
the Cabbage Moon
—J. W.

To Dr. Mouse
Sincerely, A. J.

Cabbage Moon,

Jennie loves you.

When Jennie walks in the garden,

she looks at you.

She belongs to Princess Adelgitha,
who sometimes goes there on stilts.
Princess Adelgitha does not like bones.

But they both like that old cabbage moon,
even when it hangs in sorry tatters
with shriveled leaves,
blown away by the fast South wind.

A prince once told Princess Adelgitha
the moon was a white pearl
caught in a fishnet of stars,

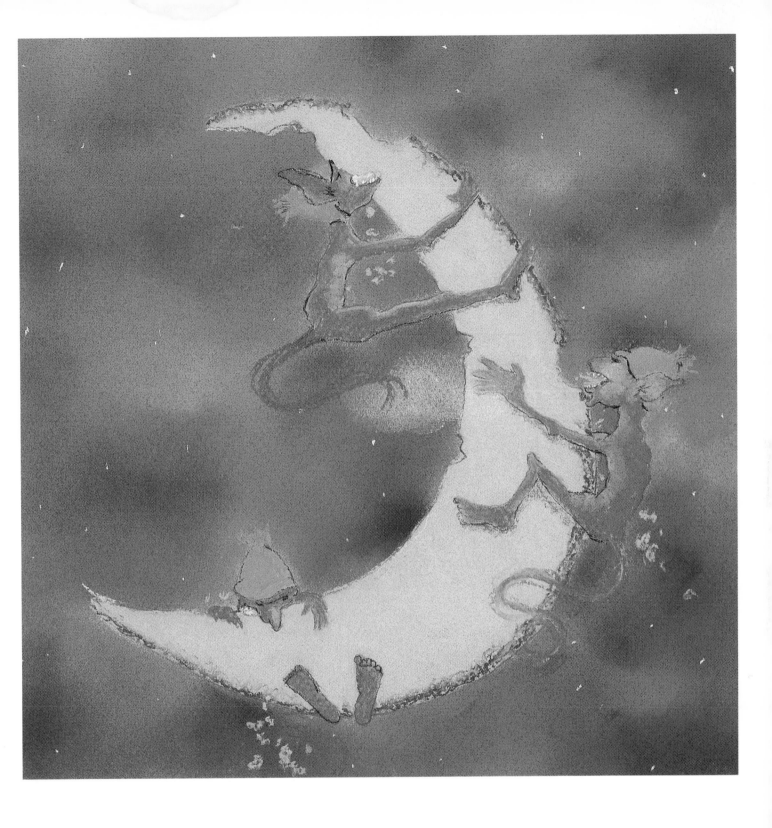

or that it was a slice of melon
eaten away by the piskies.

"Make up your mind!" she told him.
"I happen to know it is a cabbage."

Jennie knew, and the Princess knew;
and Jennie lay in the Princess's lap
and they watched happily.

One day, the cabbage moon was stolen

by a miser named Lorenzo Squink.

He lived pretty far away,

and he dashed off on a bicycle.

Princess Adelgitha chased him on her stilts
and Jennie pursued, following her nose

up and down hills,
then among the olive trees,

where in a coal-black house
that miser lived.

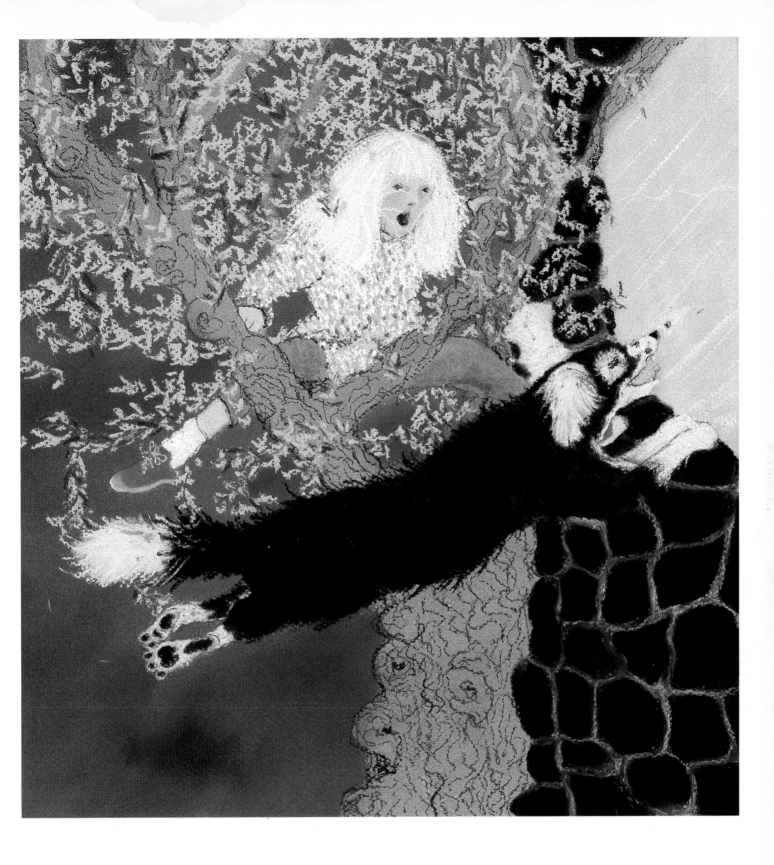

The Princess got caught on a high limb
so it was Jennie, who flew
just in time to see, through the window,
Squink fixing cabbage salad.

He was throwing nutmeg and paprika everywhere

and was about to
dip the moon into sour cream.

Jennie burst through the window

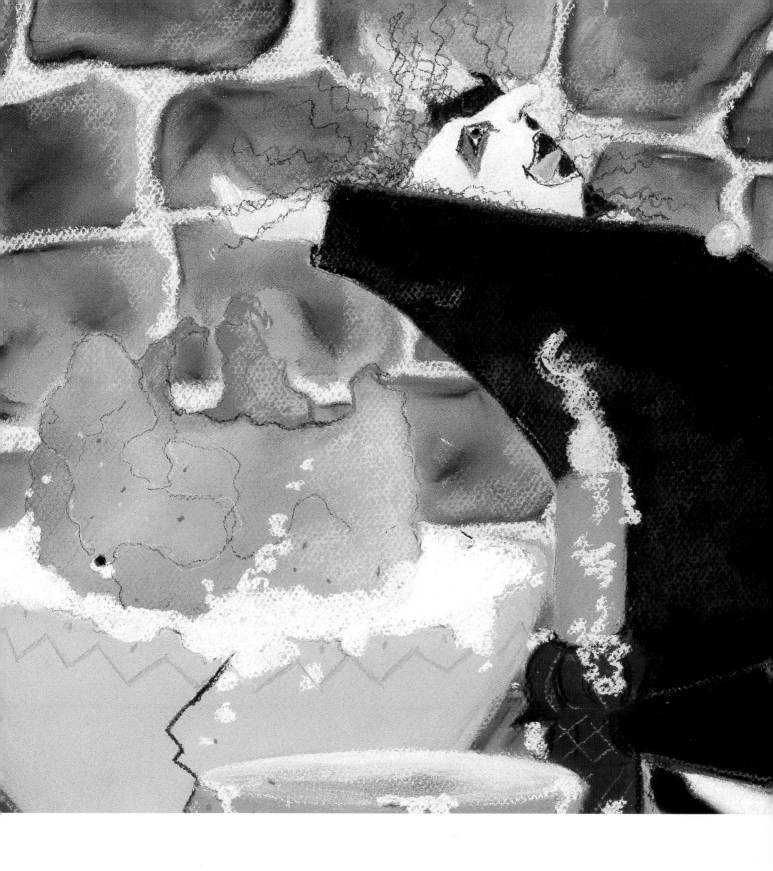

in a shower of glass—snarling!

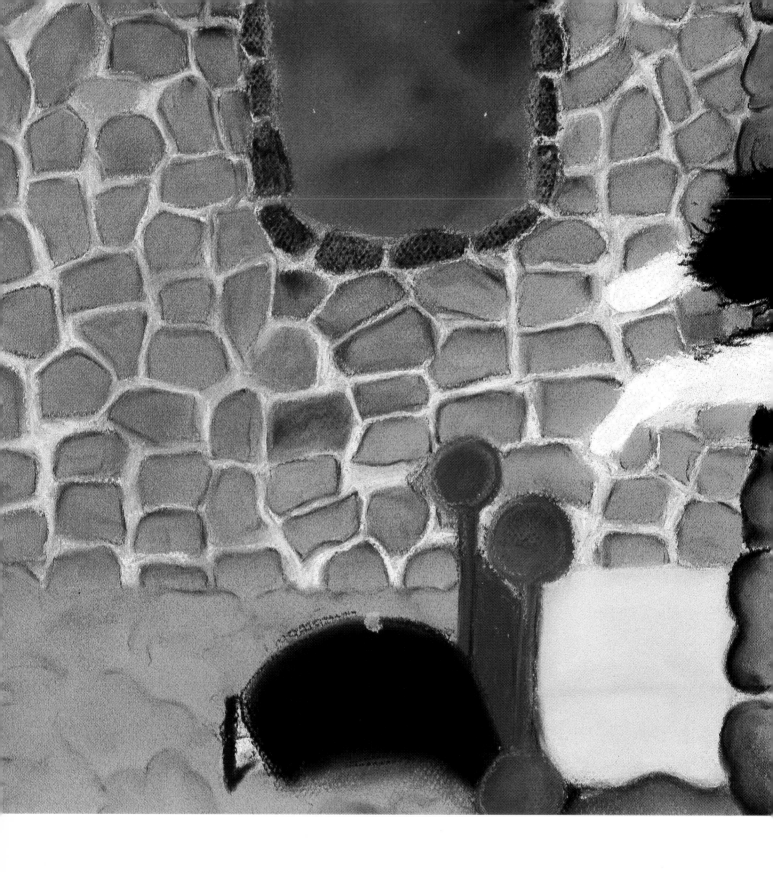

Squink hid under the bed.

Jennie gripped the moon in her teeth
and ran against the black, black sky.

Princess Adelgitha was still in the tree,
swinging and looking cross.

Jennie journeyed up the vines carefully
and tossed the trembling moon.

Adelgitha kissed it, caught it, flung it up,

and it landed, plop, in the sky.
It grew round and full once more,
and glistened green-white.